Jill Wilson

Story Link®
Program

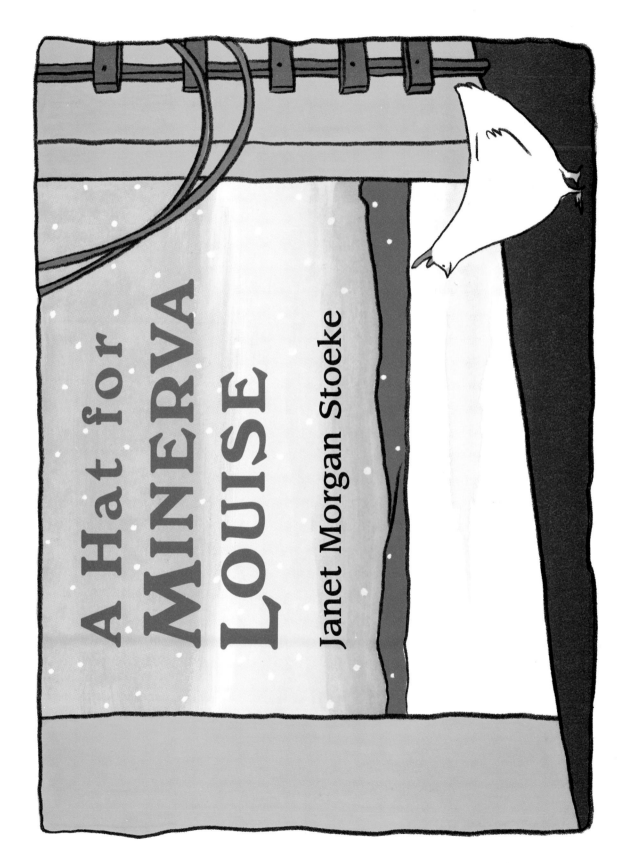

A Hat for MINERVA LOUISE

Janet Morgan Stoeke

SCHOLASTIC INC. ■ New York Toronto London Auckland Sydney

For Colin Wilcox Brooks

ISBN 0-590-12259-2

Copyright © 1994 by Janet Morgan Stoeke.
Published by Scholastic Inc., 555 Broadway, New York, NY 10012, by arrangement with Dutton Children's Books, a division of Penguin Books USA Inc.

12 11 10 9 8 7 6 5 4 3 2   7 8 9/9 0 1 2/0

Printed in the U.S.A.   08

First Scholastic printing, December 1996

Minerva Louise loved snowy mornings.

Her friends didn't like them one bit.

They stayed inside all day with their heads tucked under their wings.

Not Minerva Louise. She couldn't wait to go out exploring.

Everything was so beautiful!

She wanted to stay out all day.
But it was too cold.

If I had some warm things like you,
she said, I could stay out and play.

A scarf might help.

But not this one. It's way too big.

And these shoes are too big, too.

A hat! That's just what I need.

But not this one.

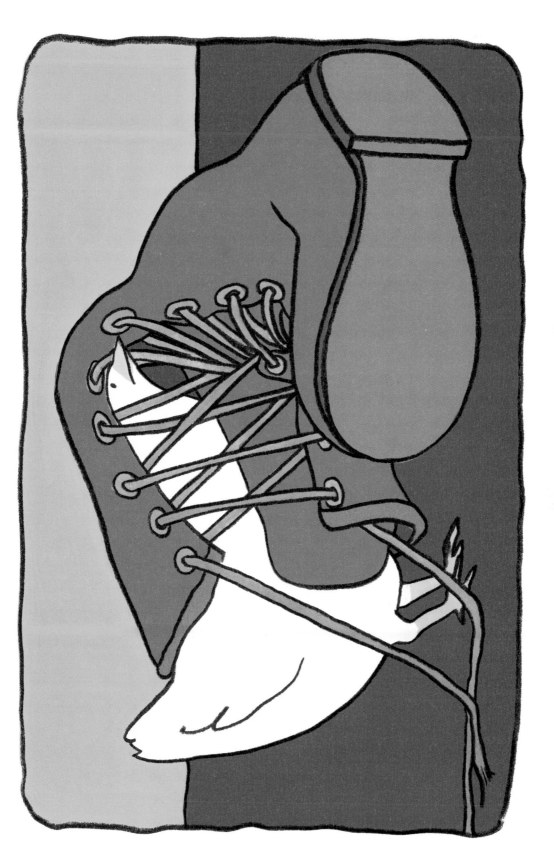

And not this one, either.
It's too heavy.

There must be a hat around here somewhere.

Minerva Louise looked outside.
Everyone had on a fluffy white hat!

Oh, your hat is wonderful!
Where did you get it?

Oh, look! What's over here?

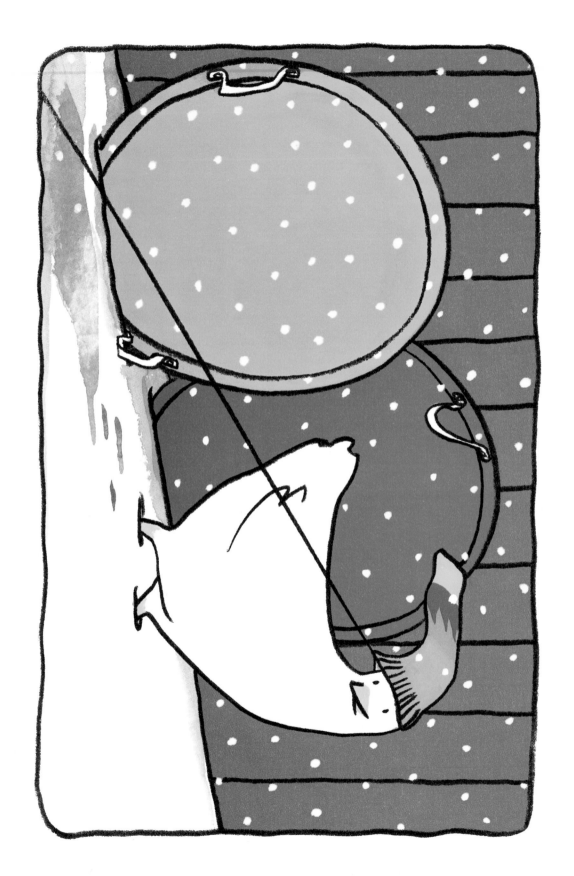

A hat! It's perfect. But what's this?

Oh, it's two hats!

which was just fine

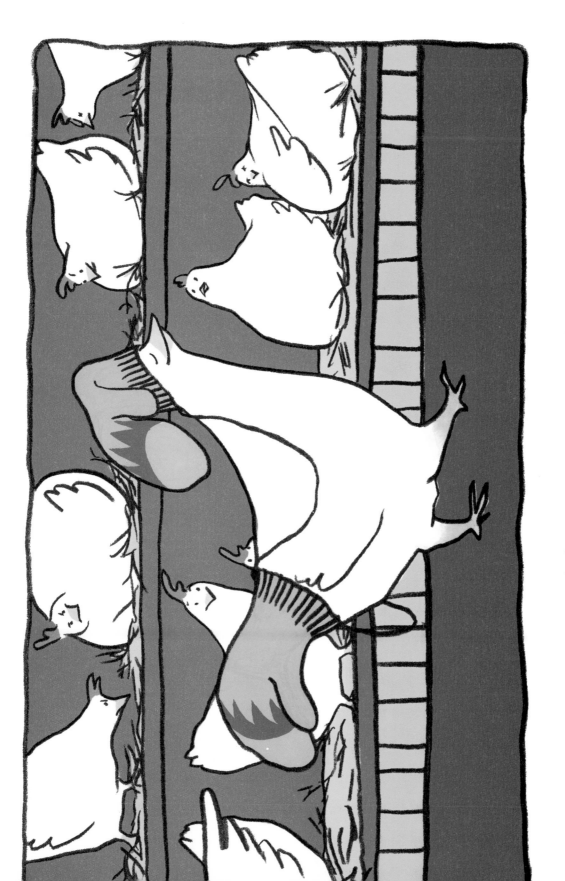

with Minerva Louise.